Doctor
Nice

Valeri Gorbachev

Holiday House
New York

HOLIDAY HOUSE is registered in the U.S. Patent and Trademark Office.
Printed and Bound in April 2015 at Tien Wah Press, Johor Bahru, Johor, Malaysia.
The artwork was created with watercolor and ink.
www.holidayhouse.com
First Edition
1 3 5 7 9 10 8 6 4 2

Library of Congress Cataloging-in-Publication Data
Gorbachev, Valeri, author, illustrator.
Doctor Nice / by Valeri Gorbachev. — First edition.
pages cm
Summary: Doctor Nice spends a busy morning helping his patients with
various winter ailments, including Moose, who caught cold after falling
through the ice, and the goat kids, who have headaches from head-butting
while playing hockey.
ISBN 978-O-8234-3203-5 (hardcover)
[1. Physicians—Fiction. 2. Medical care—Fiction.
3. Imagination—Fiction. 4. Toys—Fiction.] I. Title.
PZ7.G6475Doc 2015
[E]—dc23
2014013196

It was a busy day
at Doctor Nice's office.
The waiting room was full.

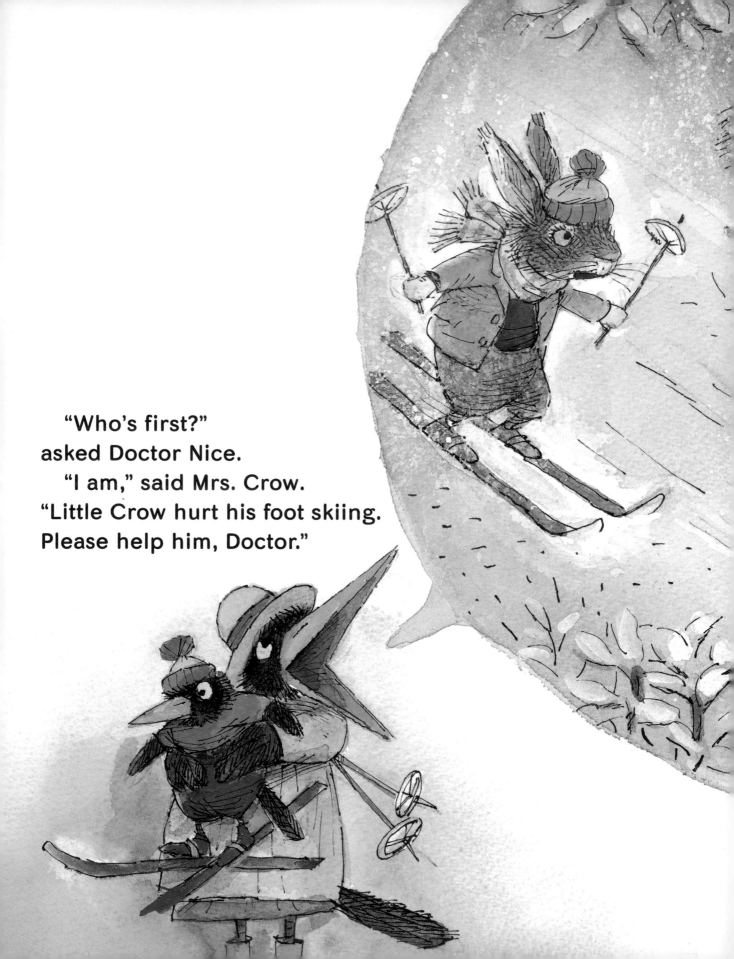

"Who's first?"
asked Doctor Nice.
   "I am," said Mrs. Crow.
"Little Crow hurt his foot skiing.
Please help him, Doctor."

"His foot is broken," said Doctor Nice.
"I will put it in a cast."

"Before long you'll be as good as new,
jumping around again," said Doctor Nice.
"I can jump right now!" said Little Crow.
"I really like my cast. Thanks, Doctor."

"Who's next?"
asked Doctor Nice.
   "I am," said Moose.
"I fell through the ice.
Achoo! Please help me,
Doctor."

"Don't worry. You just have
a cold," said Doctor Nice.

"Stay in bed for a few days, and you'll soon feel better."

"I will. *Achoo!* I will. Thank you, Doctor."

"Who's next?"
asked Doctor Nice.
  "We are," said the goat kids.
  "We were playing hockey, and
now we both have headaches.
Please help us, Doctor."

Doctor Nice checked the kids' eyes.
"You'll be fine," he said.

"These pillows will help prevent
headaches in the future."
"Hooray!" cried the kids. "Now we
can butt each other whenever we play
hockey! Thank you, Doctor."

"Who's next?" asked Doctor Nice.

"I am," said Bear. "I fell asleep in the snow, and now I have a sore throat. Please help me, Doctor."

"Let's take a look," said Doctor Nice.

"I have the perfect cure for you," he said. "Drink hot tea with this honey, and you will feel much better."

"I love your cure!" said Bear. "Honey is my favorite thing. Thank you, Doctor."

"Who's next?"
asked Doctor Nice.
"I am," said Ms. Pig.
"I just stuck my nose
out the door to see
how cold it was, and
now my nose is very
sore. Please help me,
Doctor."

"Your nose is frostbitten," said Doctor Nice. "I will take care of it.

"You have a very sensitive nose. Be sure to protect it from the cold."

"From now on I will cover it with my scarf," promised Ms. Pig. "Thank you, Doctor."

"Who's next?" asked Doctor Nice.

"I am," said Mrs. Cow. "I slipped on the icy sidewalk and hurt my tail. Please help me, Doctor."

Doctor Nice carefully
bandaged Mrs. Cow's tail.

"That should make your tail feel better," he said. "But try not to fall on it again."

"I'll be very careful," said Mrs. Cow. "Thank you, Doctor."

"Who's next?" asked Doctor Nice.

"I am," said Mommy. "It's time for lunch. Oh my, I see you've been very busy, Doctor."

"Yes," said Doctor Nice. "I had a lot of patients today. . . .

"And I helped them all."